*Tulips in those days were as precious as gold...*

# Hana in the Time

### Deborah Noyes

WALKER BOOKS

AND SUBSIDIARIES

LONDON · BOSTON · SYDNEY · AUCKLAND

# of the Tulips

illustrated by BAGRAM IBATOULLINE

*Every evening,* when Hana and Papa walked in the garden, Hana brought the little fan that Dr de Passe had given her. This was in case Papa fainted dead away on a bench.

Most evenings Papa did faint, and when he did, Hana the Renowned Physician fanned him and felt his forehead. She put an ear to Papa's chest and listened anxiously to his heart. Soon—but not *too* soon—he groaned, "What cure is there, doctor?"

Hana prescribed a kiss. Or a race to the woodpile. Or a noseful of roses.

But in the time of the tulips, Papa did not walk with Hana or faint in the garden. Like many merchants in Holland, Papa devoted himself to wanting. He wanted riches – more riches. He would not rest until he had them. And tulips in those days were as precious as gold.

$P$apa's private tulips grew beyond the fence in the North Garden. Hana and Frans, her dachshund, were forbidden to play there. When Hana was good and patient, Nurse opened the gate to show her the proud beds of red and yellow and white tulips.

In the time of the tulips, Papa spent his days at the inn, trading tulip bulbs, and his evenings with Dr de Passe and his other associates in the library. Instead of looking out through the glass doors to where Hana played among the unimportant herbs and wild flowers, the men frowned and puffed at clay pipes, peering at what looked like onions wrapped in damp paper.

"If Papa and his friends love them so," Hana asked her mother one day, "why don't the tulips make them happy?"

"Because they do not see them," Mother said. "They've forgotten altogether what a tulip is. Poor Papa," she added softly.

"Will he remember?" Hana asked.

"A tulip's beauty is great, but greed is greater. Perhaps you can talk sense to him." Mother snapped a sprig from a low bush for Hana. "Rosemary, they say, is the food of memory."

Late that night, Papa came to sit on the edge of Hana's
bed. He kissed the tip of her nose, as he did every night,
but then sighed, as if he had forgotten how to speak. Hana
pressed the rosemary into his hand.

His voice was a teasing, faraway whisper. "And what,
good doctor, do you prescribe to keep away dark thoughts?"
Hana tried to concentrate on his question, but her eyelids
drooped and closed like petals.

The next evening, Hana was sitting at her little garden table, meeting with her associates, when Nurse came to pick the burrs from her stockings. Hana begged to say goodnight to Papa indoors, but Nurse said that Dr de Passe and Rembrandt had come to call and that Hana must leave the men to their visit.

Hana liked Rembrandt because of his hearty laugh and because he brought sweets from Amsterdam to hide around the house. Once Hana had found a candied raisin under a cushion weeks after his visit. "I must see Rembrandt!" she said.

Nurse hush-hushed her.

Hana remembered something then and stopped pouting long enough to ask, "What cures dark thoughts?"

Nurse pursed her lips and scooted behind the darkening woodpile, her apron a white blur. Soon she was back. "Look here."

Hana peered into Nurse's cupped hands. "Fireflies!"

Inside, Nurse tipped the fireflies into Hana's lantern and placed a square of lace over it. All evening, they blinked behind the glass, and when Papa came, Hana said proudly, "Look. Now you have rosemary for your memory and fireflies to chase the dark away."

Papa called her his own Sleepyhead. His voice was kind, but he forgot to kiss the tip of her nose, which twitched with waiting. He motioned to a shadowy figure in the hall and seemed for an instant almost glad. "A friend has come to say goodnight."

Hana was so pleased to see her visitor that she didn't notice Papa go. "Rembrandt!"

"And how is my bright star of Haarlem?"

Hana flung her arms around Rembrandt's neck, and his soft moustache tickled her cheek.

"Have you kept to your lessons as you promised?"

"Eyes, eyes. I'm tired of drawing eyes."

"Then try something else," he said.

"What use is drawing a thing when I would prefer just to look at it?"

"You are by far my laziest pupil, Hana. There is use enough in careful study. Seeing is more than looking." He ruffled her hair and peered at the painting over her bed. "I never much liked that one."

"You don't like Papa's tulip?"

"They're the fashion – and bread and butter to some. I like any subject that gives us a means, but I'll leave the florals to others."

"What is a means?" Hana wondered aloud.

"It's money," he said. "Guilders and stuivers. It is how we painters keep our children plump."

It was Rembrandt and not Papa who kissed her nose that night. Long after he'd gone, Hana lay awake troubled by the image of Papa's unsmiling face.

In the morning, Hana raced to find Cook in the kitchen.

"What cures frowning?" she asked.

"Oh, a daisy does," Cook said firmly. Her arms jiggled as she rolled the dough. "Daisy's nothing like that vixen Tulip. She's nature's simple smile."

Hana spent all afternoon among the daisies. She plucked petals and sang:

> *"One I love,*
> *Two I love,*
> *Three I love, I say.*
> *Four I love with all my heart.*
> *Five I cast away."*

She wove Papa a whole chain of daisies.

"What's this?" Papa wondered at bedtime.

Hana held up the chain. "This," she announced, "is nature's simple smile."

Papa laughed but did not look happy. He waved at the painting on Hana's wall. Engraved on the frame were the words *Semper Augustus*. "If only your simple daisy wore *her* smile. The rarest of the rare, and worth a small fortune," he said. "Such splendour blooms only when it will, and tomorrow will be too late."

This time Papa left without even saying goodnight.

*P*apa returned early from the inn the next
day and shut himself in the library.
Associates with stern faces arrived and went out
again, waving broadsheets and scowling. Papa did
not take refreshment but sat all day long, pale and
still, in the library. Mother and Nurse and Cook
dared not disturb him.

"What's the matter?" Hana whispered.

Mother knelt and took Hana's two small hands
in her own, speaking softly. "I'm afraid it's bad
news, Hana. The tulips are worthless now and
there is no money. We have lost our means and
Papa fears for us."

Hana rushed out into the bright, clean air to find Gardener. Perhaps there was still time. "What do you do," she pleaded, "to make a flower bloom? A special flower."

Gardener balanced on his rake. He smoothed his beard. "I recommend worms," he said thoughtfully. "They give the earth its spring, its life."

Hana and Frans went to work at once. But just as Hana was about to scoop out a shiny pink worm with her spade, she saw it. Beyond the gate was a glorious, just-bloomed tulip. It was white and streaky red with feathered points, very like the tulip in the painting.

She slipped into the North Garden, her fingers itching to pick it. But that would be wrong. Even if, as Mother said, the tulips were no longer valuable, this one was so beautiful. It must be worth something.

Hana thought and thought. She watched intently the way the tulip caught the light and cupped it, swaying faintly in a breeze. And she knew what to do.

Indoors she searched her bedchamber for the parcel of tiny clay pots Rembrandt had left for her on an earlier trip to Haarlem. He had mixed the paints himself. Mother seemed relieved when Hana called her out of the too-quiet house.

Together they found an old canvas and a rickety easel that had been left in the garden shed by one of Papa's artist friends. Mother brushed the spider's webs off, and Nurse and Cook and Gardener helped Hana carry her easel and tools to the North Garden – and even left Hana and Frans alone there with the tulips. *The tulip*. The rarest of the rare.

Hana was patient all evening. Night came but Papa did not. At last, Hana crept quietly downstairs to the library. When Papa saw her, he looked away with shining eyes.

"I have something for you," she whispered.

"Perhaps another time, Hana. Papa is not well today."

"But I have found a means for us."

He leaned forward weakly in his armchair and motioned her to him. Hana held out her painting and Papa took it in unsteady hands.

"I will paint for our bread and butter like Rembrandt and his pupils. I will paint the tulips," she said, "because they are beautiful."

"Well, Hana. Would that I were as wise and brave as you are." He held the painting back and considered it. "A fine likeness. Rembrandt will be proud."

"The real one," she whispered, "is blooming now in the garden. The rarest of the rare."

A light flickered in Papa's eyes, but he shook his head. "It doesn't matter now."

"Well, then. What *will* cheer you?" Hana put her hands on her hips. "Will you never recover?"

"I may have to go back to peddling my friends' paintings, including yours," he mused. "And we will *all* have to go back to counting stuivers. But I'm not really ill, am I?"

"You said so yourself, silly."

Papa smiled for the first time in a long time. "You've missed me, Hana."

"Yes."

"And I have missed you." Papa took the little canvas from her hands and set it gently aside. He backed her up to look at her. "My goodness, I think you've grown since last I looked – really looked."

Though Hana was now determined to be a painter instead of a doctor, she reached out to feel his forehead and spoke in her most Renowned Physician's voice. "You mustn't *frown* about it," she commanded.

"What cure is there, doctor?"

Pleased that Papa remembered their game, Hana took his hand and led him through the glass doors to the garden. Rosemary perfumed the breeze. Fireflies flickered, lighting the dreams of the night. Frans sprawled under the apple tree, and, Hana knew, worms wriggled in the springy earth.

When she and Papa came to the North Garden, the tulips bowed their gorgeous, heavy heads, shy for once, in the dark.

Papa breathed the night air and squeezed her hand, and Hana knew, though he did not speak, that he would soon be well.

# Author's Note

THE FIRST DOCUMENTED CASE of market mania, tulipomania, swept through Holland between 1634 and 1637.

Imported into northern Europe in the sixteenth century and introduced to fashionable society by Konrad von Gesner, a Swiss naturalist, the tulip conquered the continent. By the early 1630s it was the ultimate status symbol, especially for rich Dutch merchants. Lavish gardens were all the rage. The bulb of a rare tulip like *Semper Augustus* might sell for a sum equal to the cost of a house or to fifteen years' wages for the average Amsterdam bricklayer. Tulip fever infected all levels of society. Tradesmen mortgaged their houses. Certain Dutch painters are said to have paid for bulbs with paintings valued today as masterpieces.

When demand rocketed, growers rushed to perfect methods for cultivating and transporting their tulips. They drove prices higher and higher. They hired guards and bought expensive insurance policies to protect their stock.

Hoping to get rich quick, everyone, it seems, took to tulip-trading. Speculation gripped the Netherlands. People used bulbs as loan collateral. Banks built special tulip vaults. But tulip fever stopped short with the crash of 1637. In a wave of panic selling, the Dutch economy collapsed, leading to mass bankruptcy and economic depression.

Tulipomania has baffled historians and economists ever since.

"Broken" or "flamed" tulips like *Semper Augustus* – resulting, we now know, from a virus carried by aphids – were valued as rare and distinct varieties in those years and are today referred to as Rembrandt tulips. Strangely enough, Rembrandt didn't favour them as a subject. The artist rarely painted florals. The term is used instead to evoke the era when he and other Dutch masters were most active.

*For Courtney Wayshak, with love*
D. N.

*For sisters Inga and Aija Terauda*
B. I.

First published 2004 by Walker Books Ltd
87 Vauxhall Walk, London SE11 5HJ

2 4 6 8 10 9 7 5 3 1

Text © 2004 Deborah Noyes
Illustrations © 2004 Bagram Ibatoulline

The right of Deborah Noyes and Bagram Ibatoulline to be identified as author
and illustrator respectively of this work has been asserted by them in accordance
with the Copyright, Designs and Patents Act 1988

This book has been typeset in Cochin

Printed in China

British Library Cataloguing in Publication Data:
a catalogue record for this book
is available from the British Library

ISBN 0-7445-5792-5

www.walkerbooks.co.uk